COURAGE

Bernard Waber

HOUGHTON MIFFLIN COMPANY BOSTON

For Helen, Isadore, Debbie, Steve, Abigail, and Sam

Copyright © 2002 by Bernard Waber

www.houghtonmifflinbooks.com

Library of Congress Cataloging-in-Publication Data

Waber, Bernard.
  Courage / Bernard Waber.
      p. cm.
Summary: Provides examples of the many kinds of courage
found in everyday life and unusual circumstances, from tasting the
vegetable before making a face to being a firefighter or police officer.
  ISBN 0-618-23855-7
  1. Courage—Juvenile literature. [1. Courage.] I. Title.
BJ1533.C8 W15 2002
179'.6—dc21

                                                    2002004065

Printed in China
SCP   21 20 19 18
4500392534

There are many kinds of courage.

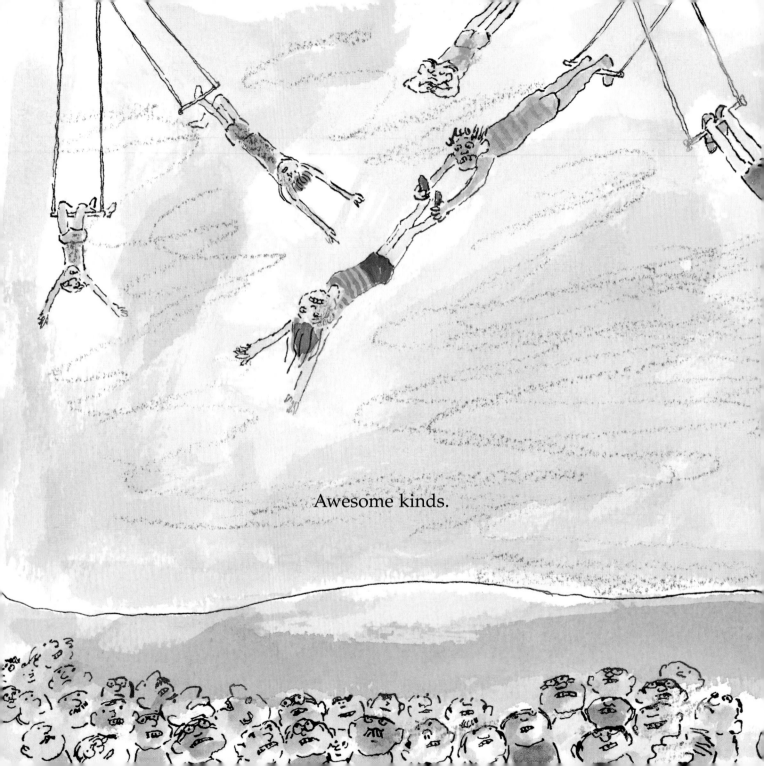

Awesome kinds.

And everyday kinds.

Still, courage is courage—
whatever kind.

Courage is riding your bicycle
for the first time
without training wheels.

Courage is a spelling bee and your word is *superciliousness*.

Courage is two candy bars
and saving one for tomorrow.

Courage is mealtime
and desperately hoping
it's not Chunky Chunks
in "real" gravy again.

Courage is nobody
better pick on
your little brother.

Courage is it's your job
to check out the night noises
in the house.

Courage is being
the new kid
on the block
and saying, flat out,
"Hi, my name is Wayne.
What's yours?"

Courage is tasting
the vegetable
before making
a face.

Courage is not peeking at the last pages
of your whodunit book to find out who did it.

Courage is
being the first
to make up
after an argument.

Courage is
deliberately stepping
on sidewalk cracks.

Courage is the
bottom of the ninth,
tie score,
two outs,
bases loaded,
and your turn to bat.

Courage is the juicy secret
you promised never to tell.

17

Courage is being sudsed
and scrubbed by strangers.

Courage is breaking bad habits.

Courage is suddenly remembering a silly joke
and trying not to giggle when everyone else
is being especially serious.

Courage is arriving
much too early
for a birthday party.

Courage is
sending a valentine
to someone
you secretly admire
and signing
your real name.

Courage is admiring but not plucking.

Courage is going to bed
without a nightlight.

Courage is deciding
to have your hair cut.

Courage is trying
to cover up
your mean, jealous side.

Courage is a scenic car trip
and being stuck in the middle
during the best part.

Courage is explaining the rip
in your brand-new pants.

Courage is
going on it
again.

Courage is
if you knew
where there were
some mountains,
you would definitely
climb them.

Courage is exploring heights—

and depths.

Courage is a blade of grass
breaking through the icy snow.

Courage is starting over.

Courage is holding on to your dream.

Courage is being a firefighter,
or a police officer.

Courage is sometimes
having to say goodbye.

Courage is what we give to each other.